27 Rue de Fleurus

(My Life with Gertrude)

Book and lyrics by
Ted Sod

Music and lyrics by
Lisa Koch

SAMUEL
FRENCH

FOUNDED 1830

NEW YORK HOLLYWOOD LONDON TORONTO

SAMUELFRENCH.COM

ISBN 978-0-573-66362-8   Printed in U.S.A.   #20719

IMPORTANT BILLING AND CREDIT REQUIREMENTS

27 Rue de Fleurus (My Life with Gertrude)
book and lyrics by Ted Sod, music and lyrics by Lisa Koch
received its World Premiere at URBAN STAGES
Frances Hill, Artistic Director, Sonia Kozlova, Managing Director

AUTHORS' BIOS

Composer and co-lyricist Lisa Koch is a Seattle singer-songwriter/actor/comedian. She has co-written such warped shows as *The Carpeters: Uncomfortably Close To You, Two's Company, I'm a Crowd,* and *Ham for the Holidays: Swine, Women and Song.* As an actor, she has appeared in *The Vagina Monologues* (Phoenix Theatre, Indianapolis), *Dirty Blonde* (Arizona Theatre Company), and as that old meany, The Wicked Witch of the West in *The Wizard of Oz* (5th Avenue Theatre). She performs regularly on Olivia Cruises, and has shared the stage with Steve Martin, Dave Brubeck, Suzanne Westenhoefer, Kate Clinton, and Janis Ian. Lisa has released four solo recordings, is a member of sketch-comedy duo Dos Fallopia, an alumnus of folk-funk quartet Venus Envy, and tours her one-woman show, *Return to Planet Lisa.* Her song, "I'm a Middle-Aged Woman" is an Internet hit (www.heylisa.com).

Librettist and co-lyricist Ted Sod's work for the stage includes: *Stealing* (O'Neill Theatre Center Music Theatre Conference, Seattle Group Theatre); *Damaged Goods* and *Not Sunset Boulevard* (Alice B. Theatre, Seattle); *Conquest of Fears* (Seattle Rep, George Street Playhouse); *Make Me Pele For A Day* (Seattle and Dallas Childrens' Theatres). His film *Crocodile Tears* (based on his play *Satan and Simon DeSoto*/Heinemann Press) was seen at the Seattle International and many other national and international film festivals and is available on DVD. Other works include: the musical *The Cousins Grimm*; the play *The Lost Art of Conversation* and the screenplay *Lucky Star.* He has directed many plays and readings; portrayed villains on all three "Law and Orders" and is currently dramaturg for the education department at The Roundabout Theatre Company in NYC. For more info: www.tedsod.com

27 RUE DE FLEURUS (MY LIFE WITH GERTRUDE) was first presented in New York City on March 6, 2008 at Urban Stages by Playwrights' Preview Productions (Frances Hill, Artistic Director and Sonia Kozlova, Managing Director). The director was Frances Hill. John Bell was musical director; Jessica Hayden was choreographer; the set was by Roman Tatarowicz; the costumes were by Carrie Robbins; lighting was by Raquel Davis; video design was by Alex Koch and the sound engineer was Daniel Margolin Lawson. The cast was as follows:

ALICE B. TOKLAS . . . . Cheryl Stern

GERTRUDE STEIN . . . . Barbara Rosenblat

PICASSO,

MABEL DODGE,

JEAN HARLOW . . . . Sarah Chalfy

MARIAN WALKER,

F. SCOTT FITZGERALD,

MAY BOOKSTAVER . . . . Susan Haefner

LEO STEIN,

SYLVIA BEACH,

VIOLET STARTUP . . . . .Emily Zacharias

PIANO/CONDUCTOR . . . . .John Bell

CHARACTERS

ALICE B. TOKLAS - petite, occasionally dry and sometimes caustic. The woman behind the woman. Madly in love with Gertrude and emotionally vulnerable. The perfect hostess to those whom she admires; not so generous with others.

GERTRUDE STEIN - robust, stout, a larger-than-life personality. She is a masculine and handsome woman. A self-proclaimed genius who speaks her own mind eloquently.

LEO STEIN - Gertrude's dyspeptic brother; has a very high opinion of himself and thinks little of Alice's relationship to his sister.

PABLO PICASSO - a famous artist whose ego is huge and who has problems understanding languages and concepts other than his own.

MARIAN WALKE - a family friend of Gertrude's from Baltimore, she is feminist who has a large family.

MABEL DODGE - the notorious narcissistic socialite/heiress and femme fatale.

SYLVIA BEACH - a no-nonsense lesbian who is proprietor of Shakespeare and Company, an English language bookstore in Paris.

F. SCOTT FITZGERALD - a famous writer who is alcoholic and has low self-esteem.

MAY BOOKSTAVER - a beauty who was Gertrude's first love from medical school at Radcliffe.

VIOLET STARTUP - a Seattle farm girl with whom Alice was smitten when she was 19.

JEAN HARLOW - the famous seductive screen siren of the 1930's who sported platinum hair. Her generation's Madonna.

DOCTOR - French, tells Alice that Gertrude's illness is grave.

PAINTINGS, WIVES

TIME

1910 and Beyond

PLACE

The mind and imagination of Alice B. Toklas

SONG ORDER/CREDITS

SALON (LET'S TALK) . . . . Ensemble
(Music & Lyrics: Lisa Koch ©1994/2006 Mamajune Music BMI)

GENIUS . . . . Ensemble
(Music: Lisa Koch / Lyrics: Lisa Koch & Ted Sod ©2006 Mamajune Music BMI)

PLACE ON THE WALL . . . . Gertrude & Alice
(Music & Lyrics: Lisa Koch ©1994/2006 Mamajune Music BMI)

I TAUGHT YOU EVERYTHING. . . . . Gertrude & Leo
(Music: Lisa Koch / Lyrics: Lisa Koch & Ted Sod ©2006 Mamajune Music BMI)

BE MY WIFE. . . . . Gertrude, Alice & Ensemble
(Music: Lisa Koch / Lyrics: Lisa Koch & Ted Sod ©2007 Mamajune Music BMI)

ROLE PLAY . . . . Alice, Gertrude & Ensemble
(Music: Lisa Koch / Lyrics: Lisa Koch & Ted Sod ©2007 Mamajune Music BMI)

VIOLETTE . . . . Mabel, Gertrude & Alice
(Music & Lyrics: Lisa Koch ©1994/2006 Mamajune Music BMI)

SALON (LET'S TALK) REPRISE #1 . . . . Ensemble
(Music & Lyrics: Lisa Koch ©1994/2006 Mamajune Music BMI)

HEMINGWAY. . . . . Ensemble
(Music: Lisa Koch / Lyrics: Lisa Koch & Ted Sod ©2006 Mamajune Music BMI)

I AM YOUR MUSE . . . . Alice with Gertrude
(Music: Lisa Koch / Lyrics: Lisa Koch & Ted Sod ©2006 Mamajune Music BMI)

DON'T, PUSSY, DON'T. . . . . Gertrude
(Music: Lisa Koch / Lyrics: Lisa Koch & Ted Sod ©2006 Mamajune Music BMI)

VIOLETTE REPRISE #1, 2 & 3. . . . . May/Gertrude/Alice/Violet/Jean
(Music & Lyrics: Lisa Koch ©1994/2006 Mamajune Music BMI)

SALON (LET'S TALK) REPRISE #2 . . . . Ensemble
(Music & Lyrics: Lisa Koch ©1994/2006 Mamajune Music BMI)

DON'T, LOVEY, DON'T . . . . Alice
(Music: Lisa Koch / Lyrics: Lisa Koch & Ted Sod ©2006 Mamajune Music BMI)

ALONE (DEAREST ONE) . . . . Alice
(Music: Lisa Koch / Lyrics: Lisa Koch & Ted Sod ©2006 Mamajune Music BMI)

AUTHORS' NOTES

The play is intended to be performed by an ensemble of women. It can be performed with as many as 12 actresses or as few as five. If you employ five, one actress plays Alice; one plays Gertrude; and three versatile women cover Leo, Sylvia and Violet; Marian, F. Scott, May and the Doctor; and Picasso, Mabel and Jean. However, you can redistribute those role assignments as you see fit. Everyone but Alice doubles as paintings and wives. These characters all have an idiosyncratic sense of humor and are highly articulate. The tempo is brisk. The musical is to be presented in one act and should run no longer than an hour and 20 minutes.

The empty frames from which the actors peer are meant to be skewed versions of the paintings in Gertrude's collection. In the original production, the set designer and director chose to dispense with traditional picture frames and opted for framed surfaces onto which video images were projected. Leo, Marian, and Picasso became the ensemble, as bride's attendants, in "Be My Wife" and portrayed voyeurs in "Role Play"; but they could just as easily have been paintings. If you choose to have the actors watch the action from the picture frames, we have prepared versions of "I Am Your Muse" with and without backups. Also, Jean and Violet brought on the dinner table at which Gertrude and Alice dine and they took on the lines of the paintings. Do what best suits your vision and budget. It can be as simple or as elaborate as you perceive the imagination of Alice being; for the action all takes place in her mind. Also, the score in the original production was played on piano – which works very well for a chamber piece – however, please feel free to add other instrumentation and orchestration.

The authors wish to thank:

Burke Pearson; Lynn Robertson; Judy Boals; Frances Hill and Urban Stages; Sarah Bay-Cheng; Hans Gallas; Karren Alenier; The Roundabout Theatre Company; Dan Wackerman and The Peccadillo Theatre Company; James Morgan and The York Theatre Company; The Annex Theatre Company and King County Arts Commission (Seattle); Rachel Friedman; Darcy Danielson; D.J. Gommels; Troy Gordon; Bruce Hurlbut; and Jillian Armenante.

This play is dedicated to all wives everywhere, no matter what their gender or circumstances and to those who wanted to marry the love of their lives and, for whatever reasons, were not able to.

(Paris, circa 1910 and beyond. The set is a reflection of the imagination and memory of Alice B. Toklas. It is not realistic. Alice's desk, typewriter and other minimal furnishings are present. There should be numerous ornate but empty frames of all sizes and shapes which represent paintings from the Stein collection and are used as doorways for entrances and exits. Occasionally, actors peer out of them and watch the action. Perhaps in some of the frames, we can see visual fragments/abstractions of 27, rue de Fleurus; 5, rue Christine; Mabel Dodge's villa; the Luxembourg Gardens; some clandestine rendezvous in America, etc.

Brief underscoring. **ALICE** *enters into a pool of light, studying her obituary)*

ALICE. "Last week, 21 years after the loss of her companion Gertrude Stein, death came to Alice Boyd Toklas, 89." Alice Boyd Toklas?! *(Reads again)* "Hemingway implied Toklas henpecked Stein." Hemingway was a pig. "Her recipe for Hashish Fudge…" Oh, dear God – not the fudge again. Who edits this nonsense? *(She reads more)* "What would Alice have been without Gertrude?" That sentence ought to read: "What would Gertrude have been without Alice?" *(Taking in the audience)* One should be allowed to write one's own obituary… don't you agree? *(She tosses it into the wastepaper can)*

My name is Alice *Babette* Toklas. *(Pointing to someone in the audience)* You think I am an imposter – yes? Well, no matter. This is the image I saw when I looked into a mirror – not the four foot, eleven chain-smoking Polish scullery maid with a moustache and a cyst on her forehead like a Cyclops. Everyone is entitled to a bit of fantasy…

Miss Stein and I were married – if you will – for almost forty years – but early on she said the most vile things

11

about me. It's all there in her impossible chicken scratch, which only I can decipher. She wrote that "I ran myself by intellect but that there was not enough intellect to go around." She called me undramatic, unimaginative, ungenerous, unconscious, remorseless, vulgar and a liar. Of course, that was before she asked me to be her "wife."

(Lights reveal **LEO**, **PICASSO**, *and* **MARIAN** *posed in picture frames as Alice introduces them)*

When I took up residence at 27, rue de Fleurus – Gertrude lived there with her brother Leo, a demented man who was always wearing his hat indoors. Once a week, she and I would listen to Leo expound on modern art and every other conceivable subject with the likes of Pablo Picasso. *(She points to him)* This is what he looked like before he went bald. Occasionally, a family friend from America would also attend. Tonight's guest is Marian Walker, an ardent feminist from Baltimore.

(ALICE *and the others sing, as they come to life and create the salon)*

SALON (LET'S TALK)

ALL.
LET'S TALK ABOUT SOMETHING BEGUILING
WITH JUST A HINT OF SEX
LET'S TALK ABOUT FEMINIST ATTITUDES AND THE
SUFFRAGETTES
LET'S TALK ABOUT STIMULATION...

GERTRUDE. *(Entering)* Intellectual, or did you have something else in mind?

ALL.
LET'S TALK ABOUT DISHES, POLITICAL ISSUES
LET'S TALK ABOUT WISHES AND DREAMS AND...
SALON

MARIAN.
REVOLUTION!

ALL.

SALON

LEO.

EDUCATION!

ALL.

SALON

GERTRUDE.

MASTURBATION

LEO.

SALON IS A SIMPLE EXCHANGE OF IDEAS IN A ROOM

GERTRUDE.

OF QUIET OBSESSIONS AND MORTAL CONFESSIONS
TO EXHUME

ALL.

THERE'S GOSSIP AND TRASH AND THE LONG LOST
ART OF LISTENING
LET'S TALK OF SALVATION AND MODERN
CASTRATION
LET'S TALK ABOUT LENIN AND FREUD AND…

(They improvise talking to one another)

PICK A TOPIC AND START A DEBATE
ORDER A CONCEPT AND DISH UP A PLATE
IT'S FOOD FOR THE MIND AND THE SOUL

NUMBER 27, AT NUMBER 27 IT'S
MANNA FROM HEAVEN, A LITTLE PIECE OF HEAVEN
AND
I DON'T REALLY HAVE A CHOICE
LOVE THE SOUND OF MY OWN VOICE

(They improvise talking to one another again)

LEO/GERTRUDE.

SYLVIA BEACH AND PAUL GAUGUIN
WHAT DO YOU THINK OF MY FRIEND CEZANNE

PICASSO/MARIAN/ALICE.

MABEL DODGE AND GERTRUDE STEIN
JOSEPHINE BAKER'S A FRIEND OF MINE

ALL.

> MARIAN WALKER, COME OUT AND PLAY WITH ME
> COME JOIN THE COTERIE WITH LOVELY ALICE B.
>
> LET'S TALK ABOUT SOCIAL UPHEAVAL AND WHAT
> WE HAD FOR TEA
> LET'S TALK 'TIL WE'RE BLUE IN THE FACE AND
> AGREE TO DISAGREE
> LET'S TALK ABOUT FARTING IN PUBLIC AND MORAL
> CENSORSHIP
> LET'S TALK OF HOUDINI, RENOIR AND PUCCINI
> LET'S TALK ABOUT JESUS AND JAZZ AND... ..
>
> SALON / NUMBER 27
> SALON / MANNA FROM HEAVEN
> SALON / NUMBER 27
> SALON / MANNA FROM HEAVEN
> SALON / NUMBER 27
> SALON!

(Everyone starts arguing passionately about cubism, etc.
LEO *trumps them)*

LEO. Impressionism, neoimpressionism, Fauvism, cubism, Dadaism, surrealism...words, words, words. I tell you, in terms of sheer power Manet does not have his equal today. Renoir, of course, has the gift of color; but he is limited intellectually. No one else really has the gift of color except perhaps Degas...

PICASSO. *(To* **GERTRUDE**, *pointing to himself)* Your brother is forgetting to mention...

LEO. I know what you are going to say, Pablo – what about Cezanne? – yes, what about Cezanne? He certainly may not be overlooked; even though he is dead; but his essential problem was mass – no one has dealt with mass like the Japanese...

GERTRUDE. Pablo says artists are forced to make something ugly when we create something new. Isn't that true, Pablo?

PICASSO. Ah, si – oui – yes. Ugly is the new beautiful!

GERTRUDE. We must all see the reality of the *late* 20th century – the past cannot help us, nor can the present – we must all see the future…

MARIAN. How does one "see" the future?

LEO. Yes, how is that possible, Gertrude – are we to be psychics now?

ALICE. Go on, Gertrude…you were saying…

GERTRUDE. Pablo and I both believe that artists must see into the future like Dr. Weininger.

LEO. Not that charlatan. For God's sake, Gertrude, the man committed suicide.

GERTRUDE. I beg your pardon. Weininger's suicide does not eclipse his profundity. We both read his book "Sex and Character" and we both thought it a very advanced way of thinking.

LEO. Bah! I never believed in that fool. He's hoodwinked you.

GERTRUDE. Is that because Dr. Weininger says we are all bisexual underneath?

LEO. Underneath what?

PICASSO. Expliquez-moi "bisexual."

GERTRUDE. If you and Matisse were to have sex with each other on one night and your wives or mistresses on another, you would be considered bisexual.

PICASSO. That cannot be so. It is impossible.

GERTRUDE. I am afraid it is so and it is possible.

MARIAN. *(To* **GERTRUDE***)* I read Weininger's book on your recommendation and I think his theories are half-baked. He says women cannot be geniuses because they don't have the requisite maleness.

PICASSO. Expliquez-moi "half-baked"?

GERTRUDE. Loco.

PICASSO. Ah, si – oui – yes. Half-baked is the new loco.

GERTRUDE. Some of us here, like Dr. Weininger, are true geniuses and a true genius always sees into the future.

LEO. Is that so?

MARIAN. Certainly it must take more than "seeing into the future" to make a genius.

GENIUS

GERTRUDE. Well, of course, Marian, it goes without saying. We geniuses are also…

EXCEPTIONAL

LEO.

UNCONVENTIONAL

PICASSO.

ARTISTIC, SYMBOLIC

ALICE.

INGENIOUS

MARIAN.

ALCOHOLIC

LEO.

IT HELPS TO BE A JEW

GERTRUDE.

I KNOW ONE WHEN I SEE ONE

ALL. *(Pointing at each other)*

AND I'M NOT… SO SURE ABOUT YOU

ALICE.

A LITTLE BELL GOES OFF, AND YOU SIMPLY KNOW
WHEN YOU ARE IN THE PRESENCE OF AN
INNOVATIVE MIND

MARIAN.

AM I A GENIUS, TOO? YES?

ALL.

NO!

MARIAN.

YES!

ALL.

NO!

MARIAN.

YES!

ALL.

NO, NO, NO, NO!

MARIAN.

WHAT MAKES A GENIUS?

GERTRUDE.

ONE WHO SEES THE FUTURE

PICASSO.

ONE WHO STUNS THE WORLD

LEO.

WITH BRILLIANT REPARTEE

GERTRUDE.

A GENIUS HAS

ALICE.

POWER

GERTRUDE.

INFLUENCE

PICASSO/LEO.

POWER

GERTRUDE.

GRACE AND

ALICE/LEO/PICASSO.

POWER

ALL.

AND A ONE-TRACK MIND

PICASSO.

DA VINCI

ALL. *(Spoken)* Genius!

LEO.

DE VEGA

ALL. *(Spoken)* Genius!

MARIAN.

MOLIERE

ALL. *(Hand motion to denote "borderline") (Spoken)* Nah…
Gifted.

MEN.

ISAAC NEWTON

WOMEN.

    MADAME CURIE

MEN.

    FRIEDRICH NIETZSCHE

WOMEN.

    CHARLOTTE BRONTE

LEO.

    ME

MARIAN.

    ME

PICASSO.

    ME

GERTRUDE.

    ME

ALL.

    ME ME ME ME ME
    WILL THEY SAY WE WERE A GENIUS
    AT WHAT IT IS WE DO?
    OR WILL THEY STILL REMEMBER US IN 1942?
    WHO WILL CALL US GENIUS IF WE DON'T PLANT
    THE SEED
    WHO ARE THEY TO JUDGE US
    JUST BECAUSE WE DON'T SUCCEED

    EXCEPTIONAL
    UNCONVENTIONAL
    ARTISTIC, SYMBOLIC
    INGENIOUS, ALCOHOLIC

    (**MARIAN** *over:* I'm a genius, don't you know)

LEO.

    THANK GOD I AM A JEW

MARIAN.

    I KNOW I AM A GENIUS

ALL.

    (SHE KNOWS SHE IS A GENIUS)

MARIAN.

    'CAUSE I'M HERE

ALL.
    WITH ALL OF YOU!

MARIAN. Go on, Gertrude, please continue.

GERTRUDE. Where was I?

MARIAN. You were talking about Jews and genius.

GERTRUDE. What more is there to say? You either are one or you aren't.

LEO. I want to challenge you on your notions about sexual attraction.

GERTRUDE. What about them?

LEO. Given your new-found lust for bisexuality – to whom are you sexually attracted?

GERTRUDE. My paintings. I just follow the passion–wherever it leads. It wouldn't be inconceivable for me to be married and living in Baltimore in five years –

ALICE. No!! That cannot be!!! *(Everyone stares at* **ALICE***)*

PICASSO. Expliquez-moi "Baltimore"?

MARIAN. *(To* **PICASSO***)* It's a city in Maryland. It's where the first Ouija board and Bromo Seltzer were invented.

PICASSO. *(Confused)* Quija? Bromo?

ALICE. Gertrude, please go on…

GERTRUDE. What was I saying?

MARIAN. You were talking about sexual attraction.

GERTRUDE. I was?

ALICE. No, you were talking about marriage and Baltimore! But I believe a Sapphist is a Sapphist is a Sapphist. *(***GERTRUDE*** gives her a look)* And we are Sapphists, are we not?

GERTRUDE. No, we are not.

PICASSO. Expliquez-moi "Sapphist."

ALL BUT PICASSO. A lesbian is a lesbian is a lesbian.

PICASSO. Ah, si, oui, yes… Sapphist is the new… *(Every shushes* **PICASSO***)*

GERTRUDE. I shall never call myself a Sapphist or a lesbian – it doesn't *mean* anything. Perhaps in order for

people to define me, it may have its purposes; but I
have bedded a he and a she during the past year...
(Everyone gasps, then speaks, overlapping one another)

ALICE. You have?!!

PICASSO. Expliquez-moi...

LEO. How is that possible?!!

MARIAN. But when do you find the time to create and
engage in love affairs, too?

LEO. *(To MARIAN)* This is one of her ploys to get attention –
she hasn't ever had...

PICASSO. Perhaps Gertrude means she is the "he," and she
has made love to herself...

ALICE. *(To GERTRUDE and the others, beside herself)* With
whom!? Which "he" have you bedded?!

PICASSO. It was not I. My mistresses would never allow it.

LEO. Certainly you don't suspect...

ALICE. *(To GERTRUDE)* Tell me!!!

GERTRUDE. The answer is somewhere in this room. *(Another
group gasp)*

PICASSO. Ridiculous!

LEO. Impossible!

MARIAN. Delectable!

ALICE. Deplorable!

*(**GERTRUDE** and **ALICE** sing their internal thoughts.
When the song begins, the others create a tableau, as if
discussing Gertrude's confession)*

PLACE ON THE WALL

GERTRUDE.

I'VE GOT THEM WHERE I WANT THEM
THEY'RE ALL WONDERING OF THE MAN IN MY BED
SPECULATING, CONTEMPLATING, FABRICATING
ON THE MAN IN MY BED TONIGHT

ALICE.

IS PICASSO YOUR LOVER TODAY?
OR MAYBE MATISSE CAME AND SWEPT YOU AWAY

THERE ON THE WALL/NOTHING TO FEAR
I WAS HOPING I COULD APPEAR IN YOUR EYES TO BE
MORE THAN A COMFORTABLE CHAIR
AH, BUT YOUR EYES…THEY LOOK RIGHT THROUGH
ME

AND THOUGH YOU'RE A PUZZLE I DON'T EXPECT TO
SOLVE
I STAND ASIDE TO WATCH YOUR PASSIONS FLOW
AND THOUGH I NEVER WOULD LEAVE YOU
YOU COULD NEVER CONCEDE THAT YOUR WORDS
ARE MY WORDS…
DON'T YOU KNOW THAT?

GERTRUDE.

ALICE B., WHERE ARE YOU?
I COULD NEVER DO WITHOUT YOU
OH, SUCH LOYALTY AND WHAT A GIFTED TYPIST
YOU MUST KNOW THAT I ADORE YOU
EVEN THOUGH I OFT IGNORE YOU
BUT THIS SALON CONVERSATION IS THE RIPEST

ALICE.

AND THOUGH YOU'RE A PUZZLE I DON'T EXPECT TO
SOLVE

GERTRUDE.

YOU KNOW THAT I'M VERY FOND OF YOU, ALICE.

ALICE.

I STAND ASIDE TO WATCH YOUR PASSIONS FLOW

GERTRUDE.

YES, I'M MORE THAN FOND, BUT LOVE IS SUCH A
SILLY WORD

ALICE.

AND THOUGH I NEVER WOULD LEAVE YOU

GERTRUDE.

DON'T YOU KNOW I'M TERRIFIED SOMEDAY YOU
MIGHT LEAVE ME

ALICE.

YOU COULD NEVER CONCEDE THAT YOUR WORDS
ARE MY WORDS…

GERTRUDE.

MY WORDS ARE YOUR WORDS...

GERTRUDE/ALICE.

DON'T YOU KNOW THAT

GERTRUDE.

I'VE GOT THEM WHERE I WANT THEM
THEY'RE ALL WONDERING OF THE MAN IN MY BED
SPECULATING, CONTEMPLATING, FABRICATING
ON THE MAN IN MY BED TONIGHT

ALICE.

A ROOM FULL OF FRIENDS AND A ROOM FULL OF
STRANGERS
AND I LOOK FOR MY PLACE ON THE WALL.
A MIND FULL OF DOUBT AND A HEART FULL OF
ENVY
AND I LOOK FOR MY PLACE ON THE WALL.
AND I LOOK FOR MY PLACE ON THE WALL.
AND I LOOK FOR MY FACE ON THE WALL.

(During the song, **ALICE** *stands behind an empty picture frame giving the illusion that she is now on the wall.* **GERTRUDE** *stares at her from afar as if she were a portrait. The others come to life as the song is ending;* **MARIAN** *and* **PICASSO** *bid adieu to* **LEO***; wave to or kiss* **GERTRUDE** *goodnight. They exit and stand behind empty frames as the action continues)*

LEO. What was *that* all about?

ALICE. *(To* **GERTRUDE***)* Yes, what *was* that all about?

LEO. *(To* **ALICE***, overlapping on "that")* Excuse me... this is a private matter between my sister and my self! *(***ALICE** *doesn't move)* Don't you have some house work to do? *(***ALICE** *exits the frame and begins to clean up; to* **GERTRUDE***)* We were having a perfectly delightful conversation about art and you found it necessary to ruin it with your ridiculous...

GERTRUDE. *(Overlapping on "your")* It wasn't perfectly delightful, Leo. It was another of your self-obsessed monologues.

LEO. I am a critic. My profession demands that I share my invaluable opinions.

GERTRUDE. You don't have a vagina, do you? *(A beat)* Well, do you?

LEO. No. Not that I know of.

GERTRUDE. Well, until you acquire one you will never know what it is to be bored. *(She starts to exit)*

LEO. You are not bisexual!

GERTRUDE. What difference would it make if I were? It's no business of yours.

LEO. It most certainly is. You live in this house with me.

GERTRUDE. And?

LEO. You have taken to acting queerly ever since Miss Toklas arrived.

ALICE. More queerly than usual?

LEO. Quiet! *(To* **GERTRUDE***)* This Alice creature does everything for you. You needn't even move. She keeps your room neat, types your scribblings, answers your letters, waits on people who call on you, plans your meals. She is the vine that is strangling the tree.

GERTRUDE. I don't see it that way.

LEO. Alice is stupid girl, Gertrude, and one day she will do harm to you.

ALICE. I am a woman, not a girl, and I am devoted to Gertrude's art.

LEO. Silence! I want you to know that any manifestation of homosexuality wreaks havoc on my digestive system and I ask you politely to refrain.

GERTRUDE. Perhaps your repulsion at the thought of two women – or two men for that matter – loving each other is in response to your own latency…

LEO. *(Stunned)* Are you saying I am a homosexual?

GERTRUDE. Where you put your penis is no concern of mine. You have often said you wouldn't have been able to function as a man if you hadn't had what was expected of you drilled into your head.

LEO. I never indulged in such palaver. Your juvenile scribblings have taken over you mind – or worse – Alice has damaged your ability to think rationally.

ALICE. If anything I have brought order to her mind.

LEO. Will you please shut up… (**ALICE** *returns to the picture frame*)

GERTRUDE. Alice has helped me immeasurably and I will thank you to stop using her as an excuse to hate my work. You are jealous of my success…

LEO. What success?!? You've had no success – any success you've had you paid for.

GERTRUDE. My books will be celebrated for years to come…

LEO. Your books are an abomination. Every one of them is a hemorrhoid.

I TAUGHT YOU EVERYTHING

GERTRUDE. At least I've written books…you only talk about it.

DILETTANTE

LEO.

DEGENERATE

GERTRUDE.

FLATTERER

LEO.

FUMISTE

GERTRUDE.

FOP

LEO.

PARASITE

GERTRUDE.

IDIOT

LEO.

PERVERT
I TAUGHT YOU EVERYTHING YOU KNOW
YOU WOULD BE NOTHING WITHOUT ME
I TAUGHT YOU ALL ABOUT THE WORLD

    FILLED WITH ART, FOOD, AND PHILOSOPHY

GERTRUDE.

    I TAUGHT YOU EVERYTHING YOU KNOW
    YOU WOULD BE NOTHING WITHOUT ME
    I BROUGHT THE LITERATI HERE
    FILLED WITH SEX, DRAMA, AND HISTORY

LEO.

    YOU ARE POSSESSIVE
    NASTY AND AGGRESSIVE
    YOU HAVE NO TASTE OR TACT

GERTRUDE.

    YOU'RE APATHETIC
    UNAPOLOGETIC
    TOO BAD YOU'RE SUCH A HACK

LEO.

    YOU'RE SO DELUDED
    YOUR WORK IS NOT INCLUDED
    NO ONE WANTS TO READ YOUR PAP

LEO/GERTRUDE.

    YOU NEVER LIKE MY WRITING
    WITH CRITICISM BITING
    I THINK WE BOTH AGREE, YOU ARE A WANNABE

    I TAUGHT YOU EVERYTHING YOU KNOW
    YOU WOULD BE NOTHING WITHOUT ME

LEO.

    YOU SHOULD CONSIDER YOU'RE A BITCH

GERTRUDE.

    AND, YOU SHOULD CONSIDER YOU'RE A QUEEN /
    DILETTANTE

LEO.

    DEGENERATE

GERTRUDE.

    FLATTERER

LEO.

    FUMISTE

GERTRUDE.

    FOP

LEO.

PARASITE

GERTRUDE.

IDIOT

LEO.

PERVERT

LEO/GERTRUDE.

I TAUGHT YOU EVERYTHING

NO, I TAUGHT YOU EVERYTHING...

I TAUGHT YOU EVERYTHING, I TAUGHT YOU

EVERYTHING ...

(Spoken) Goodbye!

LEO. I hope we will all live happily ever after and suck on our respective oranges.

GERTRUDE. Alice and I prefer cumquats. *(LEO exits in a huff.* **ALICE** *approaches* **GERTRUDE***)*

ALICE. I should be the one to leave, not your brother. I'll pack my bags this evening... *(Exiting)*

GERTRUDE. You'll do nothing of the kind! You are indispensable to me. You offer me stimulation in ways Leo cannot...

ALICE. I don't want to usurp his place in our household.

GERTRUDE. He's relinquished it. Now, we will be able to stop censoring ourselves.

ALICE. Still, he is your brother and blood is thicker than...

GERTRUDE. *(Stopping the scene)* Alice, my dear, I must interrupt. *(To us)* This never happened. My brother Leo and I never argued about Alice or my sexuality. He and I simply outgrew one another, divided the paintings and I conveniently forgot that he ever existed.

ALICE. *(To us)* Just the same, if I had moved out of 27 instead of Leo, perhaps I would have become a different person...

GERTRUDE. *(To* **ALICE***)* Is that what this is all about? What you could have been? No one forced you to live with me, you know; you accepted on your own terms...

ALICE. *(Overlapping on "own"; to* **GERTRUDE***)* When I was at school, I wanted to be a concert pianist or an author… I am sure I could have created a worthwhile work of art if I had put my mind to it…

GERTRUDE. There is no value in contemplating what could have been, Pussy, darling…

ALICE. Yes, there is, Lovey, dear! We all must make peace with the past before we die – it is a natural phenomenon.

GERTRUDE. But we are already dead. Are you trying to rewrite history?

ALICE. Why did you choose to spend your life with me? And don't tell me it was because I was a gifted typist or I shall throw that hateful machine at your swollen head…

GERTRUDE. I chose you because…I chose you because you…ahhh…what is it you want me to say, Pussy darling?

ALICE. I want you to tell us all why you chose *me* to be your "wife."

GERTRUDE. I chose you because you were…ummm…I just can't articulate it, Pussy dear. Some things are inexplicable. I do remember we were in Spain at the time.

ALICE. No, we were not. We were in Italy. And you got down on one knee and pleaded for my hand.

GERTRUDE. I did?

ALICE. Yes, you most certainly did. Once upon a time you were very chivalrous, you know.

GERTRUDE. Hmmm. *(***GERTRUDE** *gets on one knee)*

BE MY WIFE

(She sings)

BE MY WIFE, ALICE
CHANGE YOUR LIFE, ALICE
PROP ME UP AND LEND AN EAR
YOU CAN BOLSTER MY CAREER
BE MY WIFE, ALICE
GIVE UP YOUR LIFE, ALICE

I NEED A CONFIDANTE EACH DAY
TIDY UP MY DISARRAY

ALICE.

EVERY GENIUS NEEDS A LOVER AND A MUSE
CERTAINLY I'M FLATTERED, I'M THE ONE YOU
CHOOSE
BUT WHAT ABOUT ME? WHAT ABOUT ME?
MY DEAR, IF I'M WITH YOU I FEAR
THAT I WILL DISAPPEAR

GERTRUDE.

BE MY SPOUSE, ALICE
YOU'RE NO MOUSE, ALICE
SOMEONE TO ORGANIZE MY SHOES
MY AMANUENSIS, TOO

BE MY GIRL, ALICE
GIVE IT A WHIRL, ALICE
CAN'T YOU HEAR THE WEDDING BELLS
TIE THE KNOT, TWO MADEMOSIELLES

ALICE.

THOUGH I'M CLEARLY SMITTEN, I HAVE OTHER
PLANS
I ALWAYS DREAMED I'D MARRY, BUT PROBABLY A
MAN
WHAT ABOUT ME, GERT? WHAT ABOUT ME?
IF YOU I HONOR AND OBEY,
I MIGHT JUST FADE AWAY

(The paintings join in; handing **ALICE** *a bouquet and* **GERTRUDE** *a top hat)*

GERTRUDE/PAINTINGS/ALICE.

BE HER WIFE, ALICE (WHAT ABOUT ME?)
CHANGE YOUR LIFE, ALICE (WHAT ABOUT ME?)
PROP HER UP AND LEND AN EAR
YOU CAN BOLSTER HER CAREER

BE HER WIFE, ALICE (WHAT ABOUT ME?)
GIVE UP YOUR LIFE, ALICE (WHAT ABOUT ME?)
SHE NEEDS A CONFIDANTE EACH DAY
TIDY UP HER DISARRAY

ALICE.

> THOUGH SHE IS A GENIUS, SHE'LL NEED LOTS OF
> CARE
> YES, SHE'S OVERWEIGHT BUT…I'VE GOT FACIAL HAIR
> WHAT ABOUT ME, GERT? WHAT ABOUT ME?
> I GUESS THERE'S NO ONE BETTER-SUITED FOR THIS
> JOB THAN…
> *(Spoken)* Yes.

GERTRUDE. *(Spoken)* What?

ALICE. *(Spoken)* Yes. I'll be your bride.

GERTRUDE.

> BE MY WIFE, MY COMPANION, MY LOVER, MY MRS.

ALICE.

> I'LL HANDLE THE TYPING, YOU FURNISH THE KISSES

ALL.

> TIL DEATH DO US PART
> BE MY WIFE, CHANGE YOUR LIFE, BE MY WIFE, BE MY
> WIFE, BE MY WIFE

> (**GERTRUDE** *and* **ALICE** *kiss. The paintings throw rice or
> confetti.* **ALICE** *throws her bouquet;* **GERTRUDE** *her hat)*

GERTRUDE. So sentimental and sweet. If not entirely
accurate.

ALICE. It most certainly is accurate. I wasn't thinking clearly
and I accepted impetuously.

GERTRUDE. Just the same you made an excellent and intel-
ligent decision. Go on with your storytelling, my dear,
I'm sure we're all very curious to see what happens
next. But please keep in mind, post-modern audiences
expect conflict in their entertainment: car chases, gra-
tuitous violence and lots of explosions.

ALICE. Then perhaps this is the appropriate time for us to
address the subject of sex.

GERTRUDE. Which sex? Male or female?

ALICE. No, no, my dear, *our* sex – the sex we've had together.

GERTRUDE. We had sex like any loving couple – except two men, of course. When two men have sex it is nasty. I always told Hemingway that. But when two women have sex – it is divine.

ALICE. *(Referring to the audience)* Tell them – tell them about our "divine" sex life. *(To us)* I am quite sure that's why you are all here.

GERTRUDE. But Pussy, dear: Res ipsa loquitar. The thing speaks for itself. Besides, if they are truly curious about our orgasms, they can read my poetry – it's all there. In the subtext.

ALICE. Read it to them then – read "Lifting Belly." Or better yet; sing it to them.

GERTRUDE. I will not. I am not in the mood to show off my genius.

ALICE. Fine. I'm in the mood to show off mine. *(To us)* How does one sustain almost 40 years of sexual and emotional fidelity to one woman?

GERTRUDE. I give up... how?

ALICE. You must capture her attention... **(ALICE** *grabs* **GERTRUDE'S** *hand)* And hold it. **(ALICE** *squeezes her hand,* **GERTRUDE** *winces)* Tightly. *(They sing and dance)*

ROLE PLAY

MARRIED LIFE CAN BE SO VEGETATIVE
ONCE THE HONEYMOON IS DONE, YOU'VE GOT TO GET CREATIVE
AND IF YOUR LIBIDO'S GONE ASTRAY
YOU GOTTA ROLE PLAY, ROLE PLAY
GO ALL THE WAY

GERTRUDE.
FANTASY AND LOTS OF TAWDRY MAKE UP

ALICE.
SPANK HER WITH A WOODEN SPOON, YOU NEED A LITTLE SHAKE UP

GERTRUDE/ALICE.
WHISPER THINGS INDECENT AND RISQUE
YOU GOTTA ROLE PLAY, ROLE PLAY

ROLL, S'IL VOUS PLAIT

ALICE.

LAST NIGHT I WAS THE COUNT OF MONTE CRISTO
MY FOREPLAY FILLED WITH ACROBATIC LEAPS
GERTRUDE AS NAPOLEON I CAN'T RESIST, OH
SHE CONQUERED ME, THEN PROMPTLY FELL ASLEEP

GERTRUDE.

COSTUME WIGS AND LOTS OF CALISTHENICS

ALICE.

I'VE TRIED ON SO MANY HATS, I'M NEARLY
SCHIZOPHRENIC

GERTRUDE/ALICE.

EVERY GENDER, AND RELIGIOUS WAY
YOU GOTTA ROLE PLAY, ROLE PLAY
ROLL, S'IL VOUS PLAIT

(Once again, the paintings join in)

PAINTINGS.

HER MARIE ANTOINETTE WAS BEYOND SUBLIME
WHAT A WILD NIGHT WITH MATTHEW THE APOSTLE
JOAN OF ARC, SIMPLY SMOLDERING
AND HER CYCLOPS WAS UTTERLY COLOSSAL

ALICE. *(Spoken)* I once mounted Gertrude in papal robes
dressed exactly like Pope Pius The Seventh; she said:

GERTRUDE. *(Spoken)* This time Alice, you've gone too far…
I prefer Pope Pius The Eleventh"

ALL.

DON'T HUFF AND PUFF WHILE IN FLAGRANTE
DELICTO
WHEN YOU COULD SING AN ARIA INSTEAD
(AAAAAAAHHH!)

ALICE.

AND WHEN I'M DRESSED AS GARBO, I CAN PREDICT,
OH
"I VANT TO BE ALONE" WITH YOU IN BED

ALL.

MARRIED LIFE CAN BE A CONSTIPATION

IF YOU WANT TO SPICE IT UP, USE YOUR
IMAGINATION
SANTA AND HIS ELF ON CHRISTMAS DAY…

GERTRUDE. We're Jews.

ALICE. Pretend, Lovey…pretend.

GERTRUDE. *(Gives her best shot as Santa)* Ho ho ho…

ALL.

YOU GOTTA ROLE PLAY, ROLE PLAY
ROLE PLAY, ROLE PLAY
MARY PICKFORD AND GARY COOPER
AND CINDERELLA AND HERBERT HOOVER
ROLE, ROLE, ROLE, ROLE PLAY

GERTRUDE. You are just full of surprises, aren't you, Alice dear? I simply cannot imagine what you are planning for us to do next. A strip tease? Oriental contortionism?

ALICE. No, Lovey, darling, I shall be doing useful household tasks next.

GERTRUDE. These people have not come here to see you work in the garden or shop for artichokes! Why don't you tell them about your archenemy Mabel Dodge?

ALICE. But this isn't about Mabel Dodge; it's about my remembrances of *our* many years together.

GERTRUDE. I beg to differ. It is about you being the "wife of a genius"…

ALICE. That's not quite the way I would describe it…

GERTRUDE. *(Overlapping on "describe")* It says so in your own obituary: "What would Alice be without Gertrude?" Pussy darling, you know perfectly well that you discovered you were unable to share your affection for me when we were visiting Mabel's villa in Italy. You were quite possessive…

ALICE. Me? Possessive?

GERTRUDE. Yes, Pussy, dear – you wanted me all to yourself. You were a jealous green-eyed monster…

ALICE. Jealous? Of Mabel?

GERTRUDE. Yes, Mabel! In fact, you were envious of so many of my admirers, I couldn't keep track. *(Turning towards us)* Perhaps I should tell this story…when we went to the Villa Curonia in 19…

ALICE. *(Overlapping on "Villa")* No, no, no, Mabel and I shall do it. But don't go far. You'll be needed shortly. **(GER-TRUDE** *exits. To us, sotto voce)* I never cared for Mabel Dodge. She was a social butterfly in search of a golden cocoon.

(ALICE *retrieves her bag and begins doing needle work.* **MABEL** *enters with a hand mirror, primping)*

MABEL. Why are men so impossible to understand?

ALICE. Men don't know how to define themselves. That's why we women exist.

MABEL. But men are in charge of everything – how can they not be able to define themselves?

ALICE. You asked me why men are inscrutable, Mabel, and I'm trying to answer…

MABEL. I have become so adept at transforming myself into whatever I think my lover wants. I despise what I become in John's company…Edwin is another story – he is a boor. I can't transform myself when I am half asleep.

GERTRUDE. *(Entering, taking the mirror from her and handing it to* **ALICE***)* Don't fret, Mabel, dear. A femme fatale has nothing to be concerned about until she reaches 40.

MABEL. How kind of you to remind me. Do you understand men and their behavior towards women? Or better yet, do you understand women and their behavior towards men?

GERTRUDE. Men are boys grown larger. But let's not talk about them – they are quite incomprehensible and useless.

MABEL. What subject would like to investigate this after-noon, Gertrude?

GERTRUDE. You! Why don't you read to us from your new

book?

MABEL. You devil! How did you know I was writing a book?

GERTRUDE. A little bird named Alice told me. *(***ALICE** *chirps like a bird)* Intimate memoirs – are they not? *(She takes the manuscript out of Alice's bag)* Ah, quelle suprise! Here they are. *(She hands the manuscript to* **MABEL***)*. Read to us from page twelve – the passage about your school chum Violette.

MABEL. But it is meant to be a love scene – won't you read it with me?

GERTRUDE. I am sure Alice would be happy to help.

ALICE. I cannot. I am not an actress.

GERTRUDE. That is a blatant lie. You just unabashedly reveled in your talent for "role play." I want you to imagine you are Violette and you have just entered the room.

ALICE. I cannot. Please don't ask me to…

GERTRUDE. Alice, darling, don't be shy just because we are out of the boudoir. Mabel knows how passionate you are behind that placid exterior.

ALICE. But…

GERTRUDE. *(With authority)* But nothing! Do it!! *(***ALICE** *self-consciously becomes Violette and walks towards* **MABEL***)* Oh, Alice, Violette is a vixen, put some swagger in your gait. *(***ALICE** *tries unsuccessfully to be a vixen and walks towards* **MABEL** *again)*

MABEL. *(Stopping* **ALICE***)* No, no, you're wrong, Violette wasn't a vixen at all. She was from the old world – she came to me shyly, opening like a flower…

GERTRUDE. Of course, Mabel, dear. We are all innocents at that age. Alice, study your lines! *(***ALICE** *memorizes quickly what she is to say)* Ready? Begin!

ALICE. *(As Violette, with a slight French accent)* "How difficult it is to live! How will I ever go on? Oh, my tired heart!"

MABEL. "I wanted to tell her that I loved her with my entire being; but before I could utter the words, she kissed my hand *(***ALICE** *does)* and said…"

ALICE. *(Stopping the scene; to* **GERTRUDE***)* I can't continue!

Can't you see how painful this is for me?

GERTRUDE. How is it painful? It is a simple charade…

ALICE. I, too, was smitten with a girl named Violet. We were at university in Seattle together. I was 19 and she was the most glorious farm girl. She excelled at… geometry.

GERTRUDE. All the more reason to do it, I should think. Go on, breathe. Breathe, Pussy, dear, breathe…

ALICE. But…

GERTRUDE. But nothing! Your next line is…?

ALICE. "I love you."

MABEL. "And I love you."

MABEL/ALICE. She reached out her hand and laid it tenderly upon my left breast. (**ALICE/MABEL** *do*) Instantly I was attuned to the music of the finest vibration. (*They sing*)

VIOLETTE

MABEL.

SMILING… TOUCHING
WE WERE VERY YOUNG
YOU HELD MY HEART WITH ONE GLANCE OF YOUR EYES
KNOWING… LONGING
DRIFTING TENDERLY INTO A MAGIC ROMANCE
SENDING YOU LETTERS OF LOVE EACH DAY
YOU WERE A MYSTERY, MY DESTINY
VIOLETTE

MABEL/ALICE.

YOU PLAYED CHOPIN… MOVING US TO TEARS

MABEL.

I FELT YOUR PAIN AND YOUR SADNESS TOLD

MABEL/ALICE.

WAITING… BURNING
TIME IS NEVER LOST
OPEN THE GATES TO YOUR SOUL

MABEL/ALICE/GERTRUDE.

TAKING A JOURNEY WITH ONLY YOU
YOU WERE A MYSTERY, MY DESTINY
VIOLETTE

MABEL/ALICE.

THE FIRST TIME I SAW YOU I KNEW I WOULD LOVE
YOU
FOR I SAW YOUR GENIUS AND I FELT YOUR POWER
AND YOU LOOKED AT ME, AND YOU KNEW I WOULD
LOVE YOU
AND LEAVE YOU BEHIND WITHOUT BREATH OF
COMPASSION
AND YOU KNEW THE TRUTH OF THE PAST AND THE
FUTURE
　　(YOU KNEW, YOU KNEW)
AND STILL TOOK ME INTO YOUR ARMS...
HOW I LOVED YOU
SOMEDAY, WE MAY
CHANCE TO MEET AGAIN
TALK OF OUR HUSBANDS AND CHILDREN, TOO

SOMEDAY (SOMEDAY), SOMEWHERE (SOMEWHERE)
I MAY FIND THE ONE
SOMEONE TO TOUCH ME LIKE YOU

(**GERTRUDE** *approaches* **MABEL** *and gives her a look.
Grand Waltz Music.* **ALICE** *retreats or is pushed out
of the way.* **MABEL** *and* **GERTRUDE** *dance vigorously.
Just as they are about to kiss,* **ALICE** *interrupts them,
horrified*)

ALICE. Stop!! I am sorry, Mabel. I must ask you to leave
immediately.

MABEL. But you are visiting me in *my* villa. It is you that
must make a dramatic exit, not I.

GERTRUDE. Mabel, dear, don't argue. This is Alice's version
of what happened between us and we mustn't contra-
dict her.

MABEL. Come with me then, Gertrude, and I'll tell you all
about my plans to move back to America to become an
anarchist... (**MABEL** *begins to exit the room with* **GERTRUDE**

arm in arm)

GERTRUDE. You are far too wealthy to become an anarchist. A monarchist perhaps...

ALICE. Wait! You cannot leave with her, Gertrude, you must stay with me – otherwise there will be a scandal.

GERTRUDE. Forgive me, Mabel. I am not one to be indiscreet.

MABEL. I completely understand. *(She air kisses* **GERTRUDE** *and* **ALICE***)* Au revoir, mon amour. Au revoir, "Violette."

GERTRUDE/ALICE. *(Waving goodbye)* Au revoir. Au revoir... *(***MABEL** *is gone)*

GERTRUDE. *(To* **ALICE***, gently)* Pussy, my darling, I am sorry to be so blunt; but your storytelling severely lacks focus. We agreed we would introduce your guests to Mabel and your obsessive...

ALICE. *(Overlapping on "obsessive")* Focusing on Mabel was *your* idea, not mine. If there is any lack of focus, it's because you insisted I change the subject to Mabel... spending time with her wasn't...

GERTRUDE. *(Overlapping on "Mabel")* Still, you found it necessary just now to bring up the crush you had on your schoolgirl friend Violet from Seattle – is there a point to it?

ALICE. Yes, there's a point, I just haven't had the opportunity to make it yet.

GERTRUDE. Are you trying to make me envious of your infatuation with this Violet person because I brought up your jealousy of Mabel?

ALICE. I am not quite sure why I brought her up; but I'm certain there must be a subconscious reason for it.

GERTRUDE. There is only the *conscious* in art; The *sub* has nothing to do with it! Pussy, dearest, I am the writer in the family; please allow me to help. I think the next scene should be...

ALICE. *(Overlapping on "should")* No, no, no, I am quite certain of what happens next.

GERTRUDE. Excellent. Is it when I bought our first car and learned to drive – scaring half the villagers to death?

ALICE. No, Lovey, dear.

GERTRUDE. Is it when I wrote your autobiography and finally attained the fame I so richly deserved?

ALICE. No, Lovey, dear. *(To us)* The next scene takes place in 1922 or thereabouts.

GERTRUDE. 1922? Who were you envious of then? Oh yes, I am sure I can imagine.

ALICE. *(To us)* I despised having to play hostess to the wives and companions of her well-regarded friends.

GERTRUDE. But who better to entertain them? I would have bludgeoned them to death, if it were my responsibility. You had infinite patience with idle chatter…

ALICE. I did not. I only did it because you asked me to.

(F. SCOTT and SYLVIA emerge from the picture frames and take their places at the salon with GERTRUDE, singing. ALICE joins in as she hands them demitasse cups)

SALON (LET'S TALK) (REPRISE 1)

ALL.

SALON IS A SIMPLE EXCHANGE OF IDEAS IN A ROOM OF QUIET OBSESSIONS AND MORTAL CONFESSIONS TO EXHUME
THERE'S GOSSIP AND TRASH AND THE LONG LOST ART OF LISTENING LET'S TALK OF SALVATION AND MODERN CASTRATION
LET'S TALK ABOUT LENIN AND FREUD AND…

(F. SCOTT is a bit tipsy and surreptitiously puts alcohol from a flask into his cup. ALICE starts to leave)

GERTRUDE. Pussy, wait – who are these people? I don't recognize them. They don't look this way in *my* memory.

ALICE. It's F. Scott Fitzgerald and Sylvia Beach.

GERTRUDE. Do your friends know who they are?

ALICE. It's all under control, please don't fret.

GERTRUDE. Very good. Thank you, dear. *(**ALICE** exits. **F. SCOTT** and **SYLVIA** begin to debate the subject of modern manners. **GERTRUDE** interrupts them)* There are a number of people who can't help attaching themselves to meaningless ideas. They are barbarians. They have no manners whatsoever...

F. SCOTT. No manners makes me think of Hemingway – how is he these days?

GERTRUDE. Still pursuing the inaccroachable.

SYLVIA. The what??

GERTRUDE. That which is not fertile.

F. SCOTT. Poor Hemingway. *(He drinks)*

GERTRUDE. Hemingway's problem is that he is lazy.

SYLVIA. How so?

GERTRUDE. He has no discipline. He is, as I alluded to earlier, without manners. Men who go to war will never be civilized.

F. SCOTT. Every man becomes civilized between the ages of 18 and 25. And that's when Hem was in the service.

SYLVIA. I disagree. Civilization is a socialized condition – in fact, I think most artists are quite possibly...

GERTRUDE. *(Overlapping on "quite")* You are both wrong! Hemingway was uncivilized the day he was born. I had to educate him on a great many subjects including sexual intercourse and the other mysteries of life. Thank God he had the opportunity to edit my proofs – that most certainly saved him as a writer...

SYLVIA. What exactly did you teach him?

F. SCOTT. Yes, what? Tell us everything.

GERTRUDE. I will not. You know very well, Francis, that would be a betrayal of his trust.

F. SCOTT. Why do you insist on calling me Francis? I loathe and despise that name...

GERTRUDE. Take it up with your mother. Francis Scott Key Fitzgerald has an odd musicality to it...

SYLVIA. I would be mortified, too, if I were named after that dreadful man…no one can even sing his wretched anthem – *(She sings)* "Oh, say can you shit…"

GERTRUDE. Sylvia, please! Language.

SYLVIA. Oh, forgive me, exalted one. You are never vulgar.

GERTRUDE. Vulgarity is your specialty, Sylvia. You published that monstrous piece of Irish absurdity.

F. SCOTT. *(To* **SYLVIA***)* Which Irish absurdity – Shaw's?

SYLVIA. She means *Ulysses.*

F. SCOTT. Ah, yes, *Ulysses.* Let's drink to Joyce! *(He drinks)*

GERTRUDE. I shall not drink to that imposter – and neither shall you! Our sentences are far more natural than his.

SYLVIA. That "imposter's" books are selling very well. Unfortunately, Gertrude's books never sell. Would you like to buy them, Francis?

F. SCOTT. Stop callling me…whose books sell the most? Never mind. I already know. Why am I consumed with wanting more success? I'm lucky to be celebrated and wealthy when I know I am merely second rate. Let's drink to wealth. *(He drinks)*

GERTRUDE. Sylvia, you know very well that Francis and I will be read when the rest of them are dead and forgotten.

SYLVIA. Bullshit. The only one in your circle that will be remembered is Hemingway.

F. SCOTT. Sylvia is right. Hemingway will be giving an oration over both our graves. *(Drinking again)* Let's drink to Hemingway!

GERTRUDE. You are incorrect once again! Hemingway looks modern but reeks of museums.

SYLVIA. I thought you said he was a good pupil.

GERTRUDE. He was a rotten pupil. *(Sighs)* But he has magnificent eyes and a self-conscious manliness that I adore. I hate to admit it – but I have a soft spot for him.

F. SCOTT/SYLVIA. *(Sighing)* Me, too…

HEMINGWAY

SYLVIA.

> EVERY MODERN WRITER
> IS ENVIOUS, YOU SEE
> OF TOLSTOY, MELVILLE & JOYCE
> SUCCESSFUL AND ACCLAIMED
> I WOULDN'T MIND THEIR FAME
> IF GIVEN HALF THE CHOICE

F. SCOTT.

> BUT EVERY MODERN WRITER
> CONFIDENTIALLY
> HAS AN IDOL OF THE DAY
> EVERY MODERN SCRIBE
> REALLY WANTS TO BE LIKE
> ERNEST HEMINGWAY

ALL.

> A GOD AMONG MORTALS
> UNDERSTATED PROSE
> ROUGH AND TUMBLE LOOKS
> VERY MANLY CLOTHES
> NO LIMIT TO THE SUBJECTS THAT HE KNOWS

GERTRUDE.

> RECKLESS

F. SCOTT.

> AMBITIOUS

GERTRUDE.

> DRUNKEN

SYLVIA.

> DELICIOUS

ALL.

> HOW I LONG TO BE ERNEST HEMINGWAY

SYLVIA.

> HEMINGWAY'S A MAN'S MAN
> MACHO TO THE CORE
> VULGAR, OFTEN BELLICOSE
> OUTSPOKEN TO A FAULT
> PREFERS A DOUBLE MALT
> AH, HEMINGWAY'S THE MOST

ALL.

> ERNEST HEMINGWAY
> QUITE THE FISHERMAN
> BULL FIGHTER, BOXER
> CRACK SHOT WITH A GUN
> DIVORCED IN APRIL
> MARRIED IN MAY
> FULL OF SURPRISES
> HIS SUN ALSO RISES
> WHY CAN'T I BE
> ERNEST HEMINGWAY?

> *(***ALICE*** re-enters and begins her own song.* **GERTRUDE,**
> **F. SCOTT** *and* **SYLVIA** *become the wives)*

ALICE.

> WHILE THEY'RE DISCUSSING WORLDLY THINGS
> I ATTEMPT TO IGNORE THE ENDLESS
> CHATTER OF THEIR WIVES AND LOVERS
> DAY AFTER DAY...

WIFE #1.

> DO YOU KNIT?

WIFE #2.

> NO, I CROCHET

WIFE #3.

> I'M LEARNING HOW TO CHA CHA

WIFE #1.

> HAVE YOU SERVANTS?

WIFE #2.

> DO YOU COOK?

ALICE.

> I CAN BOIL WATER...

ALL WIVES.

> HA HA HA HA / HA HA HA HA

WIFE #3.

> I'M JUST HIS MISTRESS
> HE SEES ME ONCE A WEEK
> SOMEDAY HE'LL LEAVE THAT BITCH

WIFE #1.

>WHEN HELL FREEZES OVER

WIFE #2.

>YOU DON'T HAVE ANY CHILDREN?
>THAT'S REALLY SUCH A PITY

WIFE #3.

>I DON'T CARE WHAT THEY SAY, YOU'RE REALLY
>QUITE PRETTY

ALICE.

>SOMETIMES I JUST SIT AND STARE
>I'M SURE THEY THINK ME MAD
>BUT I REALLY DON'T CARE
>I SMILE AND SAY, "HOW ARE YOU, NOW?"
>"GO DROP DEAD, YOU STUPID COW"

ALL.

>HOW I LONG TO BE ERNEST HEMINGWAY
>WHY CAN'T I BE ERNEST HEMINGWAY?!

*(**GERTRUDE** breaks away and addresses **ALICE**.
F. SCOTT and **SYLVIA** exit)*

GERTRUDE. I really must put a stop to this, Alice. I assure you I never desired to be anything like Hemingway although he certainly wanted to be me…

ALICE. But…

GERTRUDE. But nothing. *(Exasperated)* I have lost my patience and I demand you tell us this instant what you are trying to say.

ALICE. I don't want to be seen for the rest of time as your appendage. I wasn't just your factotum, you know. I was much more. I was… (**ALICE** *stops herself*)

GERTRUDE. Yes? Go on. I'm listening.

ALICE. I was… (**ALICE** *stops herself again*)

GERTRUDE. Devoted to my every action, thought, feeling, word?

ALICE. Yes, perhaps I was; but that doesn't automatically make me your subordinate. I may have been your "wife"; but I was not a "wife" in the traditional sense.

GERTRUDE. Really? I see. *(They look hard at each other)*

ALICE. I am sorry, Gertrude, but you must allow me to continue telling this story the way I see fit. These next few scenes are extremely important to me...

GERTRUDE. Very well then. As you wish. *(To us)* Hopefully, we'll get to a climax soon... *(To* **ALICE***)* Now then, where am I to enter and what year it?

ALICE. *(Pointing* **GERTRUDE** *towards her entrance)* It is 1932. Right before the autobiography was published. And you are in a state. *(***GERTRUDE** *exits, to us)* Like most husbands, Gertrude believes she knows what's best for both of us and she hates not being in control. *(***ALICE** *centers herself and begins typing)*

GERTRUDE. *(Offstage, agitated)* Pussy!!

ALICE. Yes, Lovey, dear – I'm in here.

GERTRUDE. *(Enters carrying manuscript)* Pussy, darling, I think you have made more than a few careless mistakes typing the autobiography.

ALICE. Oh, no, Lovey, they are not mistakes. They are improvements.

GERTRUDE. I beg your pardon? Did you just say...

ALICE. Improvements. It's about time you started using punctuation. If you want to succeed, you must make use of the comma. And why do you insist on capitalizing America but not american?

GERTRUDE. Are you being facetious?

ALICE. I am not. I have added commas and capitalization judiciously and corrected many of the facts you remembered incorrectly.

GERTRUDE. Such as?

ALICE. The party at Picasso's. You've gotten the details of that night all confused, especially the part about Salmon eating my hat. I didn't wear a hat that evening...

GERTRUDE. I distinctly remember every aspect of that event and have written about it in scrupulous detail.

ALICE. I also had to improve on the way you have me speaking. After all, Lovey, I know better than anyone how I express myself.

GERTRUDE. Pussy, darling, I am only affecting your voice. It is really *my* voice. It may be called "The Autobiography of Alice B. Toklas"; but in fact it is not – it is about *my* life and *my* experiences.

ALICE. Whatever you write is most certainly always about *your* life and *your* experiences and I am happy that it is so. But I feel the need to clarify certain turns of phrase, especially when they are attributed to me.

GERTRUDE. Well, disabuse yourself of the need to do any such thing. It hurts my feelings.

ALICE. Nonsense. Your heart is never hurt when I criticize you – it is your vanity.

GERTRUDE. Even so, I am indeed hurt by any slight you deliberately intend. This is my book. And only I know what is best for it. I am going to take out all of your "improvements" and return every sentence to its original state. At which time, you will retype the entire manuscript and eliminate any and all "corrections." Where is my pen? I won't have you fussing about with my words or punctuation! *(***ALICE*** smiles.* **GERTRUDE** *exits, muttering to herself, looking desperately for her pen)*

ALICE. You'll come around to my way of thinking. You always do. *(***ALICE*** types as she sings)*

I AM YOUR MUSE

IT'S A CLICHÉ
TO SAY BUT
I AM YOUR MUSE

(Spoken) You know it's true…

I INSPIRE YOU
MY LOVE AND CARE ARE ALWAYS THERE
LOOKING AFTER YOU / LOOKING AFTER YOU
TYPING TIL MIDNIGHT, UP AT FIVE
KEEPING YOUR EVERY DREAM ALIVE

> PLANTING SEEDS, THEN I DEFER
> LETTING YOU BELIEVE MY THOUGHTS ARE YOURS
> I AM YOUR MUSE
>
> I INSPIRE YOU
> I DO, IT'S TRUE
> I ALLOW YOU TO BE FREE

GERTRUDE. *(Re-entering, more agitated than before, still searching for her pen)* Alice, where is my pen? (**GERTRUDE** *looks around the room for it)*

ALICE.

> WITHOUT ME YOU'D BE LOST
> YOUR SHIP WOULD BE ADRIFT
> WHERE WOULD YOU GO WITHOUT ME?
> I AM YOUR MUSE

GERTRUDE. It's my favorite pen, Alice…what have you done with it?

ALICE.

> I AM YOUR MUSE

GERTRUDE. I can't believe you lost my favorite pen! *(Exits)*

ALICE.

> GO AHEAD AND RANT
> BUT YOU KNOW DEEP DOWN
> IF IT WEREN'T FOR ME, YOU'D STARVE
> YOU WOULDN'T WRITE A SINGLE WORD
> THERE'D BE NO ONE TO PROMPT YOU
> SUPPORT YOU, STROKE YOU
> MOVE YOU, AROUSE YOU
> PROMOTE AND PROVOKE YOU

GERTRUDE. *(Entering)* Where did Alice hide you? (**ALICE** *finds it attached to Gertrude's person and hands it to her)* Ah, there you are…

ALICE.

> I AM YOUR MUSE

GERTRUDE. Get your own pen, this one's mine… (**GERTRUDE** *sits and begins making revisions)*

ALICE.

> I AM YOUR MUSE

I AM THE WOMAN BEHIND THE WOMAN
I'M YOUR SOUL AND INSPIRATION
TO CONTEMPLATE AND MEDIATE
CONJUGATE AND DEVIATE
COMPLICATE AND INNOVATE
AGGRAVATE AND FASCINATE

I AM THE WOMAN BEHIND THE WOMAN
I AM YOUR MUSE, I AM YOUR MUSE...

GERTRUDE. I'm sorry, Pussy... did you say something?

ALICE. You found your pen... I'm glad.

GERTRUDE. Why do you feel compelled to tell these people you were my muse?

ALICE. Because I was. You know very well I wasn't just your secretary. It was my life story that brought you the fame you felt you were entitled to and if it weren't for me you would have...

GERTRUDE. What? Failed? *(No response)* Oh, I doubt it, Pussy, my love. If I hadn't written *your* autobiography, I am sure I would have written someone else's to great if not greater acclaim.

ALICE. You don't mean that. You depended on me more than anyone. That's why you chose me to be your "wife." You couldn't have survived without me. Tell them! Tell I am correct...

GERTRUDE. I will not. Let them make up their own minds. They don't need us to tell them what to think. *(To us)* Do you? Don't answer that! You really mustn't pay any attention to dear, sweet Alice. I know she has been a very gracious hostess to you all, but she really has no idea how to...

ALICE. *(Overlapping on "really," trying to escort* **GERTRUDE** *out)* This is my project – this is about *me* for once, not you!!

GERTRUDE. And that is exactly why I find it necessary to intervene. I was not made to be a supporting player! And you were not meant to be the center of attention. *(***ALICE** *is silenced)* Go on, Pussy, dear, go back to your typing. *(A brief stand off.* **ALICE** *submits and begins typing violently)* It seems Alice has deliberately forgotten to tell you about the important work we did during both the world wars.

ALICE. You insisted the second one would never happen! **(ALICE** *types loudly again)*

GERTRUDE. *(Over compensating for the noise)* She's told you nothing about my political beliefs; I rather despised FDR, you know. She's also neglected to inform you of my scintillating lectures at Cambridge and Oxford, not to mention the Museum Of Modern Art. Our glorious trip to America in 1934... *(To* **ALICE***)* Will you please stop that!!?

ALICE. *(Continues typing loudly)* Sorry...can't hear you, I'm typing...

GERTRUDE. Unfortunately, Alice's sense of drama is anemic. Frankly, she is far too prosaic to be able to...

ALICE. *(Ripping a paper out of the typewriter)* Someone needs to be prosaic in this household or nothing would get done! *(Pointedly to* **GERTRUDE***)* You know which episode is coming next and you are quite frightened by being exposed, aren't you?

GERTRUDE. I am not! Please go on with your revision, Pussy. Or perhaps you'd like to go to the kitchen and supervise cook. You needn't concern yourself with us. *(To us)* Alice was a marvel in the kitchen, by the way – she fed me 'til I nearly burst. Boil water indeed... *(She laughs.* **ALICE** *glares at* **GERTRUDE***)*

ALICE. Keep in mind, Lovey, dear, this play is based on *my* memory and, like it or not, you will only be able to discuss events that I *want* you to discuss...

GERTRUDE. **(GERTRUDE** *takes this information in. After a beat; to us)* Have any of you read Hemingway's memoir – *A Moveable Feast*?

ALICE. *(Smiling)* Perfect. Continue. **(ALICE** *exits)*

GERTRUDE. *(To us, after a beat)* I am happy to report I was dead for almost 18 years when that odious book was published. I understand he tells a story about an argument he supposedly overheard while visiting us one spring afternoon at 27. This is pure Hemingway invention. Hem couldn't have possibly been in our home without us knowing it. Now, what he supposedly heard was this... *(She sings)*

DON'T, PUSSY, DON'T

DON'T PUSSY, DON'T DON'T PLEASE DON'T
DON'T PUSSY, DON'T DON'T PLEASE DON'T
I'LL DO ANYTHING PUSSY
BUT PLEASE DON'T PLEASE DON'T PLEASE...

I would never supplicate myself in such a manner. Notice he was unable to relate what Alice was saying to motivate such fear in me. Hem says that Alice was saying things "unlike anything he had ever heard before." This from a man's man. Such nonsense!

*(**ALICE** re-enters wild-eyed, with a stack of letters and a manuscript)*

ALICE. What are these?!!

GERTRUDE. What are what, Pussy, dear?

ALICE. I was cleaning out the cupboards and I found these love letters addressed to you.

GERTRUDE. Give them to me.

ALICE. I will not! Who wrote these to you?

GERTRUDE. I can't possibly answer you unless you let me read them.

ALICE. Have you more than one admirer I am not aware of?

GERTRUDE. You know I am only fond of you.

ALICE. Then who is May Bookstaver?

GERTRUDE. May Bookstaver is now Mrs. Charles Knoblauch...she helped me find a publisher for my book *Three Lives*.

ALICE. *(Appalled) She* wrote these to you?!?

GERTRUDE. Pussy, darling, our history is archaic. I have quite forgotten about her and you should too...

ALICE. How can I? In the same cupboard was this scandalous manuscript. You've written in graphic detail about your lust for her... *(Reading from manuscript)* "The pain of passionate longing is very hard to bear...I am now convinced that my longing for you is genuine and loyal..."

GERTRUDE. You're taking it out of context, Pussy, dear. It's true May Bookstaver inspired the manuscript – but it isn't *about* her. Besides, it's never been published. No one knows about it.

ALICE. Is she your muse?

GERTRUDE. Don't be ridiculous – I am my muse! There is no muse to inspire me other than my self!! We've been through this over and over. *May* I please see the letters?

ALICE. *(Losing control)* How dare you speak her name in our home??

GERTRUDE. But Pussy, darling, I was only requesting if I *may* see...

ALICE. Again you torment me! Never speak or write her name in my presence. Are you still in love with her?

GERTRUDE. Certainly not.

ALICE. I don't believe you – these letters are filled with your undying devotion to her! *(She begins to rip the letters to pieces,* **GERTRUDE** *speak/sings)*

GERTRUDE.

DON'T PUSSY DON'T
DON'T PLEASE DON'T
DON'T PUSSY DON'T
DON'T PLEASE DON'T

ALICE. You *are* still in love with her! She means more to you than I do!! Why have you deceived me all these years?!! This manuscript and the autobiography will never be published. And you will never see me again. *(She begins violently ripping the pages of the manuscript)*

GERTRUDE.

I'LL DO ANYTHING PUSSY

BUT PLEASE DON'T
PLEASE DON'T PLEASE

ALICE. *(Overlapping)* The more you protest; the more I will destroy!! You will never write her name again – do you understand?? *(**ALICE** threatens to rip rest of the manuscript to shreds. **GERTRUDE** nods her head slowly; **ALICE** is back in control)* Now, sit!! Sit down now and retype every *may* to *can.*

GERTRUDE. But…

ALICE. But nothing! Every single solitary *may* will be changed to *can* – now!! Do it or I will destroy every last page of the Autobiography as well. *(She starts to rip the pages of the Autobiography **GERTRUDE** was revising. **GERTRUDE** wails, as if her child is being murdered)*

GERTRUDE.
DON'T PUSSY
DON'T DON'T
PLEASE DON'T

ALICE. Then type! Now!! And don't stop until every you-know-what has been changed to can.

GERTRUDE. *(As if speaking to an insane person)* Even when it refers to the month?

ALICE. Yes. It seems to me you have always much preferred June or July to…

GERTRUDE. May. *(**ALICE** screams upon hearing May's name; **GERTRUDE** is not quite sure how to handle the situation)*

ALICE. Type! *(**GERTRUDE** begins to hunt and peck painstakingly. **ALICE** watches for a bit and then addresses us, as the lights fade on **GERTRUDE**)*

ALICE. I couldn't bear the idea of Gertrude being in love with any one but my self. It is true I succeeded in banishing most of those who threatened me; but no matter how hard I tried to forget about Gertrude's love affair with you-know-who, she was always there to torment me.

*(**MAY** enters with a parasol as **GERTRUDE** types. **ALICE** watches the action from a picture frame)*

MAY. Are we alone?

GERTRUDE. *(Confused)* I think so.

MAY. That shrew didn't follow you?

GERTRUDE. Not this time. *(To MAY)* Who are you? *(Stopping the scene; to ALICE)* Who is this, Alice? I am confused – is this Marian or…

ALICE. It is that painted harlot you professed your love to in letter after letter…

GERTRUDE. You want me to pretend this meeting between us really happened?

ALICE. Yes.

GERTRUDE. *(Rolling her eyes to us. To MAY, playing along)* Oh, May, my darling…I missed you terribly.

MAY. I never stop thinking of you.

GERTRUDE. Nor I you.

MAY. How difficult it is to live! Oh, my tired heart!

GERTRUDE. You are here with me now, dearest one. I will repair your heart.

MAY. I love you so.

GERTRUDE. And I love you.

> *(Bell tone. She puts her hand on MAY's breast and MAY puts hers on GERTRUDE's as they sing)*

VIOLETTE (REPRISE)

GERTRUDE/MAY.
> THE FIRST TIME I SAW YOU I KNEW I WOULD LOVE YOU
> FOR I SAW YOUR BEAUTY AND I FELT YOUR POWER
> AND YOU LOOKED AT ME, AND YOU KNEW I WOULD LOVE YOU
> AND LEAVE YOU BEHIND WITHOUT BREATH OF COMPASSION
> AND YOU KNEW THE TRUTH OF THE PAST AND THE FUTURE
> AND STILL TOOK ME INTO YOUR ARMS
> HOW I LOVED YOU…

*(**GERTRUDE** and **MAY** kiss. Alice reacts.)*

ALICE. Stop!! Stop!! I cannot bear to watch such disloyalty! Get out, get out, you painted strumpet! Leave my house this instant and never return!! *(**ALICE** chases **MAY** around **GERTRUDE**. **MAY** screams and grabs her parasol which she uses as a weapon to ward off **ALICE**. **ALICE** grabs it and they are holding opposite ends of the parasol – a tug of war ensues)*

GERTRUDE. *(Trying to keep them apart)* But we aren't in the house, Pussy – we're in some bizarre part of your remarkably fertile imagination. *(**MAY** finally gets the parasol away from **ALICE** and jabs at her with it as if it were a foil)*

MAY. *(Blowing a kiss to **GERTRUDE**)* Au revoir, mon amour. *(To **ALICE**)* Au revoir, couchon! *(**MAY** snorts like a pig)*

ALICE. *(Going after **MAY** again)* Wait! Don't move, you hussy! How can you brazenly carry on like this in front of me?

GERTRUDE. *(Separating them; holding **ALICE** back as **MAY** scampers upstage)* It's all a fabrication of your fevered brain, Pussy. You even have May looking like Marian and believe me, that was not the case. I swear to you – I never saw May after she left me for another woman and then married a man – it's all there in the manuscript. *(She looks at the manuscript in pieces on the floor)*

ALICE. I couldn't bring myself to finish the manuscript.

GERTRUDE. Don't you see how silly this is? I could just as easily imagine you having a surreptitious rendezvous with your school chum Violet.

ALICE. I haven't seen Violet Startup in 40 years.

GERTRUDE. Violet Startup – was that her name? How bucolic.

*(**VIOLET STARTUP** enters)*

VIOLET. Alice! I missed you terribly! Seattle has never been the same since you left. Please come back to me!

ALICE. But I live with Gertrude in Paris now...

VIOLET. She doesn't appreciate you. I will. I will adore you the way you adore her...please come back to me – I will abandon my husband and eleven children.

ALICE. Dear God, why did I ever leave you behind? You meant the world to me...

(Bell tone. She puts her hand on **VIOLET***'s breast,* **VIOLET** *put her hand on* **ALICE***'s breast and they both sing)*

VIOLETTE (REPRISE 2)

ALICE/VIOLET.
THE FIRST TIME I SAW YOU I KNEW I WOULD LOVE YOU
FOR I SAW YOUR BEAUTY AND I FELT YOUR POWER
AND YOU LOOKED AT ME, AND YOU KNEW I WOULD LOVE YOU
AND LEAVE YOU BEHIND WITHOUT BREATH OF COMPASSION
AND YOU KNEW THE TRUTH OF THE PAST AND THE FUTURE
AND STILL TOOK ME INTO YOUR ARMS...

ALICE. *(Breaking from* **VIOLET***'s embrace)* But Violet Startup and I never did anything with one another. We were never lovers.

GERTRUDE. Exactly my point. This sort of destructive day-dreaming is endless. You can imagine me with hundreds of other women if you choose to – why not an affair between me and Jean Harlow?

*(***JEAN HARLOW** *enters)*

JEAN. Gertie, you nit wit. I was readin' one of your books the other day...

GERTRUDE. Shut yer face, ya no good tramp. What book?

JEAN. Who can tell? They're all the friggin' same – repetition, repetition, repetition and none of that crap you write makes sense.

GERTRUDE. Then go get yourself another girlfriend if you don't like readin' my crap.

JEAN. I can't – I'm addicted to your breasts.

(Three bell tones, as all hands move to breasts. **JEAN** *puts her hand on* **GERTRUDE***'s breast,* **GERTRUDE** *puts her hand on* **MAY***'s.* **MAY** *puts her hand on* **VIOLET***'s breast and* **VIOLET** *puts her hand on* **ALICE***'s, etc., and so forth. They all sing)*

VIOLETTE (REPRISE 3)

JEAN/ALICE/VIOLET/GERTRUDE/MAY.
THE FIRST TIME I SAW YOU I KNEW I WOULD LOVE
YOU
BLAH, BLAH, BLAH
FOR I SAW YOUR BEAUTY AND I FELT YOUR POWER
BLAH, BLAH, BLAH
AND YOU LOOKED AT ME, AND YOU KNEW I WOULD
LOVE YOU
BLAH, BLAH, BLAH
AND LEAVE YOU BEHIND WITHOUT BREATH OF
COMPASSION...

ALICE. Stop! Enough!! All of you go away. *(Everyone including* **GERTRUDE** *begins to exit)* Not you, Lovey. *(They all stop)*

VIOLET. *(Running and kneeling in front of* **ALICE***)* I knew you still cared for me!

ALICE. I meant Gertrude. *(***GERTRUDE** *moves to* **ALICE,** *as the others exit and become part of the empty picture frames once again)*

GERTRUDE. Pussy, dear, can't you comprehend that May never loved me the way I wanted her to?

ALICE. But you were in love with her. You were madly in love with someone other than me, were you not?

GERTRUDE. It was a very long time ago. Res ipsa loquitar. The thing speaks for itself...

ALICE. Still, I wanted to be your first love – you led me to believe I was.

GERTRUDE. I never intended to hurt you.

ALICE. And yet you have. Damn you, Gertrude Stein. You

lied to me.

GERTRUDE. I did nothing of the sort. I just didn't speak of her existence.

ALICE. That is tantamount to lying.

GERTRUDE. You never spoke of Violet Startup, isn't that the same thing?

ALICE. No, it's not the same thing at all.

GERTRUDE. (**GERTRUDE** *moves to* **ALICE**) You're being unreasonable, Pussy, it *is* the same thing.

ALICE. Go away! Before I do something rash. I have half a mind to leave you. (**ALICE** *grabs the papers of the Autobiography again*) Or better yet, I should burn all your precious words.

GERTRUDE. *(Frightened)* Don't, pussy, don't... don't, please don't... .

ALICE. Don't what? Leave you or burn your precious words? *(Silence.* **GERTRUDE** *looks away)* Get out of here... Go! *(A beat.* **GERTRUDE** *leaves, shaken. To us, as she picks up the mess she has made earlier)* I made Gertrude's life miserable. I never forgave her for May and she finally told me if I didn't stop punishing her she would leave *me.* It got to the point that I contemplated murder. Or suicide. Or both. But who to kill first? Gertrude, May or myself? I had built my entire identity around being Gertrude's "wife" and I felt terribly betrayed when I realized there was a time she had given her love and passion to another.

We moved from 27, rue de Fleurus to 5, rue Christine. I know all the biographies say we were evicted by the landlord to make way for his newly married son; but the truth is I could no longer live in the place where I had discovered Gertrude's love of that scarlet woman. Our lives had changed. Fewer guests were tolerated and the notorious salons at 27 were finished.

(A reprise of Salon [Let's Talk], at a slower tempo. A dinner party for two. A long table which is exquisitely set,

is rolled into place by **GERTRUDE**. *The ensemble sings from the empty picture frames. One of the picture frames is conspicuously missing or covered with black cloth.* **GERTRUDE** *is wearing a beautiful Japanese kimono – she hands another to* **ALICE** *who puts it on before she sits.* **GERTRUDE** *dines as she speaks)*

SALON (LET'S TALK) (REPRISE 2)

PAINTINGS.
> PICK A TOPIC AND START A DEBATE
> ORDER A CONCEPT AND DISH UP A PLATE
> IT'S FOOD FOR THE MIND AND THE SOUL

GERTRUDE. I do not understand why a Negro would want to be called "colored." I dislike it when instead of saying Jew people say Hebrew or Israelite or Semite. A Negro is a Negro is a Negro and…

PAINTINGS. …A Jew is a Jew is a…

GERTRUDE. *(Cutting them off)* Einstein is the creative philosophic mind of the century and I am the creative literary mind of the century.

ALICE. The century isn't over.

GERTRUDE. There is talk that *The Autobiography of Alice B. Toklas* will be made into a Hollywood film; but I am aghast at the probable casting – who will play you? Norma Shearer? Who will play me?

PAINTINGS. Spencer Tracy. *(***GERTRUDE** *gives the paintings a look)*

GERTRUDE. Hemingway wrote me a letter. In it, he says that he had always wanted to fuck me. *(***ALICE** *drops her fork)* He also says that you, Alice, were threatened by any of my real men-friends. I wrote back to him and said: "Anyone who marries three girls from Saint Louis hasn't learned much."

ALICE/PAINTINGS. Hemingway. *(They spit)* Pttuuu!

GERTRUDE. Spit all you want. He obviously lusted after me. Probably still does. *(***GERTRUDE** *returns to her meal. To*

ALICE) This soup has such a piquant flavor – do you recognize it?

ALICE. I do not. I am not eating the soup. Cook made it especially for you.

GERTRUDE. I must tell him it is magnificent. *(A beat. Reaching for* **ALICE***'s hand)* I am so content to be here with my furniture and paintings, Pussy, darling…all the things I hold so dear to my heart.

PAINTINGS. What happened to the Cezanne? It was your favorite painting of all and now it is missing.

GERTRUDE. We are eating the Cezanne.

*(***GERTRUDE*** suddenly grabs her stomach as if she has been poisoned. She stares at* **ALICE** *and then staggers about writhing in pain.* **ALICE** *is distraught;* **GERTRUDE** *moans loudly)*

ALICE. Dear God! Gertrude, what is it?!! Cook, cook – vite, vite, hurry!! Something terrible has happened to Madame Stein!!

*(***GERTRUDE*** is assisted getting into her chair by* **ALICE***; her breathing is labored.* **ALICE** *takes off* **GERTRUDE***'s kimono and places it on the back of her chair. The dining table is removed)*

GERTRUDE. *(Overlapping the above action, moaning loudly)* Oh, my stomach – the pain – Alice, the pain is unbearable – help me – help me – I can't breathe. I cannot breathe. Alice, please help…help me…*(Stopping the scene. To* **ALICE***)* You are not going to make me die again – are you? It was miserable enough the first time.

ALICE. I am sorry, my dear. But I couldn't possibly finish this story without including your demise.

GERTRUDE. Very well. If you insist… *(***GERTRUDE*** immediately resumes moaning. A* **DOCTOR** *appears, pulls* **ALICE** *aside and whispers to her sotto voce)*

DOCTOR. Your friend is gravely ill, Madam. We believe it is cancer of the stomach. We must operate immediately; but we cannot operate until she regains her strength.

GERTRUDE. *(To* **DOCTOR***, opening her eyes)* I order you to operate now – I was not made to suffer.

DOCTOR. We will do our best, Madame Stein. *(The* **DOCTOR** *exits)*

GERTRUDE. *(To* **ALICE***, who is frightened)* This may be the end for me, Alice.

ALICE. Gertrude, please forgive me – I should have taken better care of you.

GERTRUDE. Nonsense. You were the perfect wife.

ALICE. But, I never wanted to... *(Frightened)* Oh, dear God...

GERTRUDE. I have taken care that you will be provided for.

ALICE. How will I ever live without you? I will be lost. I will be irretrievably lost.

GERTRUDE. We must learn to do everything, Alice. Even to die.

*(***ALICE*** kneels in front of* **GERTRUDE** *and sings, pleading)*

DON'T, LOVEY, DON'T

ALICE.

DON'T LOVEY
DON'T DON'T
PLEASE DON'T
DON'T LOVEY
DON'T DON'T
PLEASE DON'T

I'LL DO ANYTHING LOVEY
BUT PLEASE DON'T PLEASE DON'T PLEASE

*(***GERTRUDE*** drifts off)*

ALICE. *(To us)* I know that all the books about Gertrude say her last words to me were:

GERTRUDE. *(Semiconscious)* What is the answer? What is the answer?

ALICE. *(To us)* I, of course, was mute and Gertrude continued...

GERTRUDE. In that case, what is the question? *(***GERTRUDE** *expires)*

ALICE. But that is not what really occurred.

GERTRUDE. *(***GERTRUDE** *again stops the scene)* It isn't??

ALICE. No, it isn't. *(To us)* What Gertrude actually said was:

GERTRUDE. *(Becoming semiconscious again)* What is the question? What is the question?

ALICE. *(To us)* To which I wanted to reply: "Do you love me as much as I love you?"; but instead I stood mute. Gertrude continued…

GERTRUDE. If there is no question, then there is no answer.

> *(***GERTRUDE** *expires. A few beats. ***GERTRUDE** *rises, crosses to* **ALICE** *and waltzes romantically with her in silence. ***GERTRUDE** *kisses* **ALICE** *tenderly and exits. A repeat of the brief underscoring from the opening)*

ALICE. *(To us)* Gertrude's cancer was inoperable. She was pronounced dead at 6:30 pm on July 27, 1946. My life was altered in so many ways without her. I no longer had someone who was completely dependent on me for everything. "What would Alice have been without Gertrude?" indeed.

I decided to work relentlessly to insure that her artistic legacy be honored.

I saw to it that Gertrude's unpublished works were published. Even the book about May. That wasn't easy. I wrote two cookbooks and my memoirs – why not? I needed the money.

I stayed on at Rue Christine until I was evicted. Unfortunately, Gertrude's family never acknowledged me as her "wife." And the laws did not protect me.

But friends came to the rescue – they always do.

Do I regret choosing to be wife of a genius? I have often contemplated this question, and, of course, the only answer I can come up with is:

The thing speaks for itself.

(She sings; sitting in Gertrude's chair and wrapping herself in Gertrude's kimono)

ALONE (DEAREST ONE)

DEAREST ONE
I'M THINKING OF YOU
OH, HOW ARE YOU TODAY?
DEAREST ONE
I MISS YOU STILL
AH, THE WINTER IN PARIS
IS BRUTAL AS EVER
AND I AM ALWAYS COLD
MY BODY IS FEEBLE
TWENTY-ONE YEARS
AND I'M STILL THINKING OF YOU
EVERY DAY, EVERY NIGHT
WHEN ONE IS OLD
ONE REMINISCES
I MISS THE GARDENS,
THE SALONS, YOUR KISSES AND...

DEAREST ONE
I AM SO LONELY
YES, I MAY JOIN YOU SOON
DEAREST ONE
I CAN'T WAIT TO SEE YOU
AND YOU'LL TALK MY EAR OFF
WHILE I HOLD YOUR HAND
PLEASE WAIT FOR ME
WAIT FOR ME...
YOUR DEVOTED
ALICE B.

*(***GERTRUDE*** appears in her own light in an empty frame. They connect, as the lights fade)*

PROPERTY & COSTUME PLOTS

Properties Plot

Preset:

Alice's desk and chair

Working manual period typewriter and onionskin paper

Wastepaper can

Period tote bag with Mabel's manuscript and Alice's needlepoint

Gertrude's notebooks from which Alice types

Gertrude's chair and side table

Three additional chairs for guests

Hand and Costume props:

Newspaper with obituary (Alice)

Tea tray with service for 5 (Serving tea was part of the choreography in "Salon/Let's Talk") (Leo to Alice)

Plate with mimed cookies (Serving cookies was part of the choreography in "Salon/Let's Talk") (Alice)

Dust rag (Optional – Alice cleaned up during the argument between Leo and Gertrude)

Wedding bouquets and top hat – (Leo, Picasso, Marian entered with 4 bouquets – Marian gave one to Alice; the others each had one during "Be My Wife" choreography. Picasso also concealed top hat which was given to Gertrude)

Tote bag with Mabel's manuscript and Alice's needlepoint inside (Alice/Gertrude)

Period hand mirror (Mabel)

2 demitasse cups/saucers (Sylvia/F. Scott)

Flask (F. Scott)

Three long silk scarves (F. Scott, Sylvia, and Gertrude put on scarves to become the wives as part of the choreography in "Hemingway/Wives")

Typewritten manuscript of *The Autobiography of Alice B. Toklas* (Gertrude)

Pen (on Gertrude's person)

Typewritten/yellowing *QED* manuscript and numerous love letters (These are destroyed every night and must be replenished daily) (Alice)

Parasol (May Bookstaver)

Fully set table with elegant dinner service for two (In the original production there were real plates, glasses and silverware; but food and drink were mimed) (Gertrude and Alice)

Kimonos (Gertrude and Alice)

Costume Plot

ALICE B. TOKLAS
Elegant calf-length dress with print over-blouse and coordinated jacket
  or sweater
Tasteful jewelry/accessories
Adds: Japanese kimono

GERTRUDE STEIN
Satin blouse
Embroidered vest
Long tweed skirt
Broach
Adds: Japanese Kimono

MARIAN WALKER
Conservative and tasteful day dress, circa 1911-1913

MABEL DODGE
Fashionably eccentric ensemble for entertaining at home, circa
  1910-1913

SYLVIA BEACH
Mannish skirt, tailored blouse and blazer, circa 1922-24
Beret

MAY BOOKSTAVER
Smart day dress with slight bustle, circa 1898
Parasol

VIOLET STARTUP
Simple peasant blouse and full-length cotton skirt with belt, circa 1890's
Small lace cap

JEAN HARLOW
Extravagant satin gown with fur or marabou trim and matching or coor-
  dinated floor-length over-jacket, circa 1932
Long pearl necklace

LEO STEIN
Conservative men's suit circa, 1911-13
Black derby

PABLO PICASSO
3-piece suit with cravat and two toned shoes, circa 1911-13

F. SCOTT FITZGERALD
Lightweight summer/linen suit, circa 1922-24

DOCTOR.
Long white lab coat over suit and tie

Glossary

FLEURUS (pronounced FLERR–OOZE)
DR. WEININGER (pronounced VINE–INGER)
FUMISTE (means chimney sweep; pronounced FOO–MEESTE)
VIOLETTE (pronounced VEE–OH–LET)
SALMON (pronounced SAL–MAHN)
COUCHON (pronounced KOO-SHOWN)
VITE   (pronounced VEAT)

Resources

The following books/videos/websites were very valuable in creating this musical and in the original production:

THE AUTOBIOGRAPHY OF ALICE B. TOKLAS
GERTRUDE STEIN

THE THIRD ROSE (Gertrude Stein And Her World)
JOHN MALCOLM BRININ

CHARMED CIRCLE
JAMES R. MELLOW

GERTRUDE AND ALICE. DIANA SOUHAMI
TWO LIVES: GERTRUDE AND ALICE. JANET MALCOLM

GERTRUDE STEIN: WHEN THIS YOU SEE REMEMBER ME
A FLIM BY PERRY MILLER ADATO

HANS GALLAS' WEBSITE:
http://www.gertrudeandalice.com/receive.html

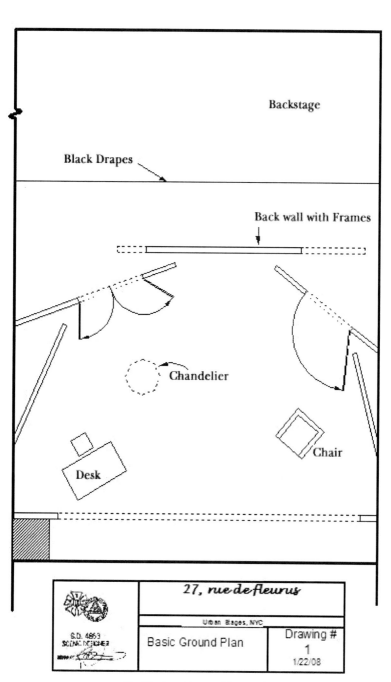

Set Design: Roman Tatarowicz

Set Design: Roman Tatarowicz

From the Reviews of
27 RUE DE FLEURUS
(MY LIFE WITH GERTRUDE)...

"*27 Rue de Fleurus* gets its sweetness from a genuine love of its subject, the "marriage" of Gertrude Stein and Alice B. Toklas. The music is well handled by John Bell; and the all-female cast sings excellently."
– *Village Voice*

"What we have here is a love story, fraught with jealousy and passion like others, but most of all, it celebrates the incredible bond between two women who decided to share their lives, even during a time when it was relatively unheard of. That alone makes *27 Rue de Fleurus* worth an evening of your time."
– *GO Magazine*

"Ms. Rosenblat, who, seated, resembles portraits of Stein, plays Gertrude as a commanding bully. And Ms. Stern's Alice is a bright, attractive creature. ("Everyone is entitled to a bit of fantasy," she says.) They're strong, plausible performances."
– *NY Times*

"Credit Ted Sod and Lisa Koch, writers of *27 Rue de Fleurus*, with the provocative notion of fashioning a revisionist musical from Alice B. Toklas' corrective version of her life with literary giant Gertrude Stein. Name-dropping opening number "Salon (Let's Talk)" sets the smart tone for the musical's mise en scene – the Parisian apartment at 27 Rue de Fleurus where Gertrude (Barbara Rosenblat) and her companion Alice (Cheryl Stern) preside over a fashionable literary salon that attracts artists and writers of international renown, as well as the occasional American feminist and Hollywood movie star. It's an inviting scene, to be sure."
– *Variety*

"This is Alice's turn, Alice's attempt to put herself center stage and give her version of being "the woman behind the woman." The show's opening has a genuine brightness as Alice introduces herself as a transformed glamorous creature, the Alice she wanted to see in the mirror. We enter the salon of 27 Rue de Fleurus, where Alice has come to live and Gertrude bluntly sings, "Be my wife, Alice/Give up your life, Alice." The two opening songs — "Salon (Let's Talk)" and "Genius" — glow with good humor and witty lyrics and set the salon as the place to be. As well as Picasso and Fitzgerald, it's also the scene for Mabel Dodge, Sylvia Beach, Marian Walker, and even Jean Harlow."
– *Backstage*

"Bookwriter Ted Sod, who collaborated on the lyrics with Lisa Koch, have both done the most important thing right: They've made Stein and Toklas human beings who are struggling through the confines of a marriage, with Stein "playing" the husband, and Toklas the wife. Koch sure likes to write waltzes; not since *Night Music* has a score contained so many. But they're all lovely-to-beautiful. The opening is a good deal of fun, because the waltz plays against all the ungainly subjects Gertrude, Alice, and their guests discuss."
– *Theatremania*

Printed in the United States
207121BV00005B/1-114/P